BEEZY
AND
FUNNYBONE

stories by Megan McDonald

illustrated by Nancy Poydar

ORCHARD BOOKS • NEW YORK

Orchard Books, A Grolier Company
95 Madison Avenue, New York, NY 10016

Manufactured in the United States of America
Printed and bound by Phoenix Color Corp.
Book design by Helene Berinsky

The text of this book is set in 20 point Stempel Garamond.
The illustrations are gouache painting reproduced in full color.
10 9 8 7 6 5 4 3 2 1

Library of Congress Cataloging-in-Publication Data
McDonald, Megan.
Beezy and Funnybone / stories by Megan McDonald ;
illustrated by Nancy Poydar.
    p. cm.
Summary: Presents three stories in which Beezy and her dog have
adventures on the ground and in the air.
ISBN 0-531-30211-3 (trade : alk. paper)
ISBN 0-531-33211-X (library : alk. paper)
ISBN 0-531-07161-8 (paperback : alk. paper)
[1. Dogs Fiction. 2. Florida Fiction.] I. Poydar, Nancy, ill. II. Title.
PZ7.M478419 Bf 2000   [E]—dc21   99-24698

For Louise, Annie,
and Eliza

—M.M.

Contents

Fetch

"I'll teach you how to fetch,"
Beezy told Funnybone.
"I throw the ball.
You bring it back.
FETCH!" said Beezy.
She threw the ball.

Funnybone ran after the ball.

Funnybone ran away with the ball.

Funnybone dug a hole
and buried the ball in the dirt.

Beezy found a stick.

"FETCH!" she called.

Funnybone ran after the stick.

Funnybone ran away
with the stick.

Funnybone dug a hole
and buried the stick in the dirt.

Beezy threw ball after ball,
stick after stick.
Funnybone ran away
and buried them all in the dirt.
"Funnybone! You'll never
learn to fetch!" said Beezy.
Beezy walked away.
Funnybone brought
a ball to Beezy.
Funnybone brought
a stick to Beezy.
"Good dog!" said Beezy.
"You fetched!"

Then Funnybone
could not stop fetching.
He fetched the newspaper.

 He fetched
Beezy's baseball glove.

He fetched Gran's car-washing rag.

"Okay," said Beezy.
"We know you can fetch now."

Funnybone did not stop fetching.

He went next door and

fetched Mrs. Stark's slipper.

Beezy took it back.

He fetched Mr. Reed's geranium.

Beezy took it back.

He fetched Tabby's toy mouse

and King's big bone.

Beezy took them back,
even though King
made her nervous.

"All this fetching
is making me tired," said Beezy.
"I'm going to get the mail.
Today's the day I get invited
to Sarafina's birthday party."

Beezy looked in the box.

No mail!

"Gran!" said Beezy.

"There's no mail today."

"You got your card
from Sarafina!" said Gran.
"I put it on the table.
On the porch."
Beezy looked on the table.
No card.
Beezy looked on the chair.
No card.
Beezy looked
on the porch floor.
No card.

"That's funny," said Gran.

"Maybe it blew away."

"Arf!" said Funnybone.

"Not now," said Beezy.

Beezy and Gran looked

in the grass.

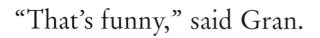

Beezy and Gran
looked under the car.

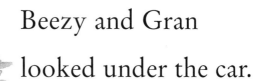

Beezy and Gran looked
in the garden.

Funnybone dug and dug in the dirt.

16

Funnybone fetched something
between his teeth.
He brought the thing back to Beezy.
It was a small white envelope
with dirt and tooth marks all over it.
"Look who delivered
the mail today!" said Gran.
"Funnybone!" said Beezy.

The Spat

Beezy's teacher read a story.

Beezy's teacher said "spat."

"Did you say spit?" asked Beezy.

"I said spat," said Mrs. Derby.

"What's a spat?" asked Merlin.

"It's your homework today.

Find out what it means."

"Give us a clue," said Beezy.

"One hint," said Merlin.

"It has to do with babies,"

said Mrs. Derby.

On the bus,

Beezy and Merlin asked Sarafina,

"What is a spat?"

"A spat is spit," said Sarafina.

"Is not," said Beezy.

"Is too," said Merlin.

"Not!" said Beezy.

"Too!" said Merlin.

"But it has to do with babies," said Beezy.

"Babies spit," said Sarafina.

On the way home,

Beezy and Merlin asked Mr. Gumm,

"What is a spat?"

"A spat is part of an old shoe,"

said Mr. Gumm.

Old shoes

did not have anything

to do with babies.

Beezy and Merlin went
to the library to look for a spat.
"What is a spat?"
Beezy and Merlin asked
the man behind the desk.

The man looked in the dictionary.
"A spat is a little fight
between friends," said the man.

"That's not it," said Beezy.

"Is too," said Merlin.

"The man said."

"But babies don't fight,"
said Beezy.

"Let's go home," said Merlin,
"before we have a little fight
between friends."
Funnybone ran down the walk
to meet Beezy.
Funnybone was carrying
some flowers in his mouth.

"Funnybone!" said Beezy.

"Were you digging
in Gran's garden again?"

"Looks like Funnybone picked me
some flowers," said Gran.

"I'll put these in water."

"Wait!" Beezy told Gran.

"There's an ooey, gooey oyster
on your flowers!"

"Wait!" said Merlin.

"There's an uggy, buggy slug
on your flowers!"

"Never mind," said Gran.

"It's just a spat."

"What did you say?" asked Beezy.

"What did you say?" asked Merlin.

"It's a spat. A spat is a baby snail.

See? She's just starting
to grow her shell."

"Baby snails have to do
with babies," said Merlin.
"Gran," said Beezy,
"you are better than
the dictionary."

Funnybone Sees the World

At last! The day of Sarafina Zippy's birthday party.

"Arf!" said Funnybone.

"Yes. You can come too," said Beezy.

"If you promise *not* to fetch.

And no Key lime pie for you.

Just birthday cake!"

Beezy and Merlin

wrapped the present.

A hula hoop!

"It looks like a giant pizza!"

said Merlin.

"It looks like a flying saucer!"

said Beezy.

At the party,
they played circus games
like lion tamer
and walk-the-tightrope.

Then Sarafina took Merlin

and Beezy and Funnybone

to the circus grounds

for a ride in a hot-air balloon!

The man in front of the big basket

was dressed up

in old-timey clothes.

He had on a round hat,

a vest with a gold watch chain,

and funny shoes.

"Spats!" said Beezy and Merlin,

pointing to his shoes.

Funnybone jumped
right into the basket.
Sarafina stepped in after him.
"Me first," said Beezy.
"Me first," said Merlin.
"Let's not have a spat," said Merlin.
He let Beezy go first.

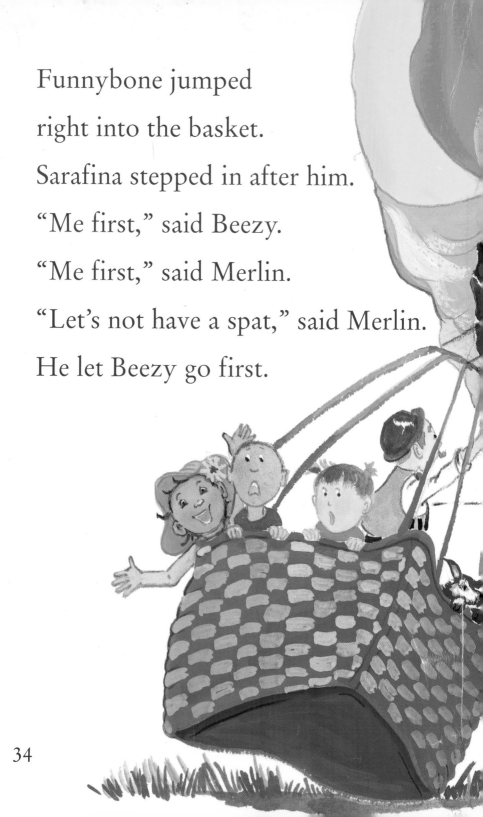

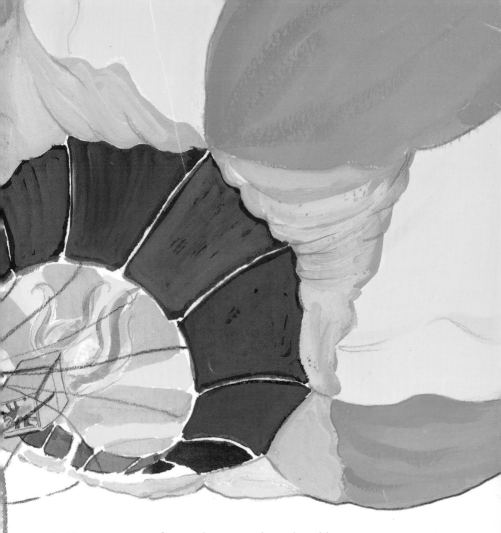

The man fired up the balloon.

WHOOSH!

"Yikes!" yelled Beezy.

"Yikes!" yelled Merlin.

The basket tipped.
Beezy almost
fell over.

The basket jolted.

Merlin's insides did flip-flops.

"Hold on!" said Sarafina.

Beezy and Merlin did not hold on.

Beezy and Merlin

jumped out of the basket.

Sarafina ran after them.

"C'mon! You get to go up and up,

higher than trees!

All the people look like ants.

All the houses look like candy corn.

And the cars look like fleas

in the flea circus."

"You go," Beezy told Sarafina.

"I'll be an ant."

"And I'll be candy corn,"

said Merlin. "Or a flea."

WHOOSH!

All of a sudden,
the balloon started to float
up, up in the air.

"Wait for us!" Sarafina called.

"Funnybone!"

Beezy jumped up and down
and waved her hands.

"WAIT!" they cried.

"He's going up!" said Sarafina.

"Isn't he scared?" asked Merlin.

"Funnybone! Come back!"
cried Beezy.

"I'll buy you Key lime pie.
The thing you like best
in all the world.

I'll let you fetch the mail,
and you don't even have
to bring it back!"
"Arf!" said Funnybone,
wagging his ears and waving his tail.
Funnybone floated up and up,
higher than the trees.

Funnybone's head was in the clouds.

Funnybone was flying!

"Arf! Arf!" said Funnybone.

Funnybone was no bigger

than a pencil point

in the blue, blue ocean of sky.

"FUN-NY-BONE!"

yelled Beezy and Merlin and Sarafina

at the top of their lungs.

At last, the balloon man

let out the air,

and Funnybone drifted
down, down, down,

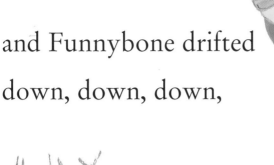

left, then right,

right, then left,

to the ground.

"Funnybone!
Don't ever fly away again!"
Beezy hugged him hard and
rubbed his belly.

"Did you see the whole town
of Soda Springs?" Sarafina asked.
"Funnybone saw
the whole state of Florida!"
said Merlin.

"Funnybone saw

the whole wide world!"

said Beezy.